Sammy was no good at parties.
This one was like all the others.

Everyone bounced in and had fun,
except Sammy. He was too shy.
"I want to go home,"
said Sammy.

Tiger

written and illustrated by
Jane Johnson

Andersen Press
London

GW 2615173 1

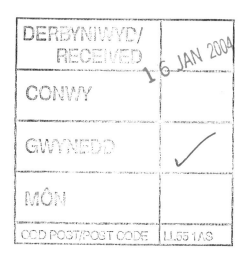
Copyright © 2002 by Jane Johnson
The rights of Jane Johnson to be identified as the author and illustrator of this work
have been asserted by her in accordance with the Copyright, Designs and Patents Act, 1988.
This paperback edition published in 2003 by Andersen Press.
First published in Great Britain in 2002 by Andersen Press Ltd., 20 Vauxhall Bridge Road, London SW1V 2SA.
Published in Australia by Random House Australia Pty., 20 Alfred Street, Milsons Point, Sydney, NSW 2061.
All rights reserved. Colour separated in Italy by Fotoriproduzione Beverari, Verona.
Printed and bound in Italy by Grafiche AZ, Verona.

10 9 8 7 6 5 4 3 2 1

British Library Cataloguing in Publication Data available.

ISBN 1 84270 244 0

This book has been printed on acid-free paper

But a corner over there was quiet.
Magic was happening.
A lady was painting faces.

Sammy went nearer to watch.

She could make you whatever you wanted to be.
"Are you ready?" she asked Sammy,
and he nodded, "Yes."

He closed his eyes and felt her fingers
stroke his face. They were so soft,
he was almost asleep.

"You can look now," she said.
And Sammy saw he was a tiger –
big, beautiful and bravest of creatures.

"You're a tiger!" said the parrot.
"Yes."
"What do tigers do?"
"Um . . ." said Sammy.

Then he knew. Tiger roars and claws;
his tail goes swish and he snarls.
"Tiger is Lord of the Jungle,"
said Sammy proudly.

The others nodded and wished they were tigers, too.
"What do you do?" asked Sammy.
"Um . . ." they said. They didn't know.

"Parrots squawk and flap their wings,"
said Sammy.

"And lizards dart and hide," said the lizard.
"Yes!" shouted Sammy.

Suddenly everyone
was calling to Tiger.
"Look, Tiger, squirrels climb!"

"See me flying – I'm a butterfly!"

"I'm a panther, look how I leap!"

"What do I do?" whispered a very small frog.
"Frogs hop," said Sammy gently,
and showed him how.

All the creatures ran and shrieked,
and chattered and sang,

and Tiger roared his majestic roars,
until they were tired.

Then they ate their favourite things,
and when they were full . . .

. . . everyone grew quiet and slept.

Through the stillness of his sleepy jungle,
Sammy heard calling and clapping . . .
"Tiger! Where's Tiger? Step forward,
the Lord of the Jungle!"

"A prize for Sammy the tiger!"

"We'd better be going. It's been a long day,"
said the parents, finding their children.
"I want to stay," said Sammy.

So he did,

'til the very . . .

. . . END